WHEN
BLOOD
LIES

WHEN BLOOD LIES

Linda L. Richards

RAVEN BOOKS
an imprint of
ORCA BOOK PUBLISHERS

Library and Archives Canada Cataloguing in Publication

Richards, Linda, 1960–, author
When blood lies / Linda L. Richards.
(Rapid reads)

Issued in print and electronic formats.
ISBN 978-1-4598-0837-9 (paperback).—ISBN 978-1-4598-0838-6 (pdf).—
ISBN 978-1-4598-0839-3 (epub)

I. Title. II. Series: Rapid reads
PS8585.I1825W53 2016   C813'.54   C2015-904516-9
C2015-904517-7

First published in the United States, 2016
Library of Congress Control Number: 2015946332

Summary: In this work of crime fiction, gossip columnist Nicole Charles buys a desk at auction that turns out to be at the center of a secret from the past and a crime in the present. (RL 4.8)

Orca Book Publishers is dedicated to preserving the environment and has printed this book on Forest Stewardship Council® certified paper.

Orca Book Publishers gratefully acknowledges the support for its publishing programs provided by the following agencies: the Government of Canada through the Canada Book Fund and the Canada Council for the Arts, and the Province of British Columbia through the BC Arts Council and the Book Publishing Tax Credit.

Cover design by Jenn Playford
Cover photography by Peter Rozovsky

ORCA BOOK PUBLISHERS
www.orcabook.com

Printed and bound in Canada.

19 18 17 16 • 4 3 2 1

The problem with putting two and two together is that sometimes you get four, and sometimes you get twenty-two.

—Dashiell Hammett

ONE

These days there are times when I can't even remember what made me get into the news business in the first place. I know I wanted to do some big thing. I wanted to make a difference. Change things. I wanted to know that every day when I got out of bed, the work I did would have a positive impact on many lives.

And so I played with ideas.

There were other possibilities, but none of them made sense for me.

I don't like being around blood, so being a doctor, nurse or veterinarian was out of the question, even though I like animals. And sometimes people.

Teacher? While I don't dislike kids, the thought of being cooped up in a classroom with a bunch of them every day didn't sound like a fun.

Cop? I don't like violence. I don't like guns. I know there is more to the job than that, but I couldn't get past those basics.

Firefighter? Of course what they do is worthwhile. They do great work. But it looks so very difficult all the time. Like, you have to sweat and lift a lot of heavy stuff. I'm not particularly talented at either of those things.

But I'm "good with words," or so I was always told. And I know how to "turn a phrase." I thought about being a novelist but found I didn't really have much to say. (Maybe someday.) And then, reading through the descriptions of programs at a local college, a two-year journalism program caught my eye.

In the first place, it was the only two-year program in the field west of Toronto. And to be honest, it sounded super fun. I would learn *how to dig for information, write a compelling news story, conduct an illuminating interview* and *other important skills*.

And suddenly it all made sense. I knew that of the things I *could* be, nothing else had ever really clicked for me. Journalism became, in an instant, the only true thing I'd ever wanted to pursue.

I applied to the program. Got accepted. Then spent the next two years learning about how I was going to make a difference. For maybe the first time ever, my life had meaning. I couldn't wait to graduate.

I did my practicum at the *Vancouver Post*, my hometown newspaper as well as one of the top papers in the country. I was on my way. But right in the middle of my internship, the society columnist dropped dead (no mysterious causes). And I just walked into his job.

It was either a lucky break or a curse. Three years later, I'm still not sure which. The work is not difficult, but it's also not what I imagined. When I signed up to be a reporter, I thought I'd be running around chasing down leads and uncovering conspiracies. Investigating stuff. Busting things wide open. (I wasn't sure what kind of things, but still, it's what I dreamed.)

As the gossip columnist, what I *really* do is go to pretty parties and take photos of pretty people. Then I write pretty words about them to go under the photos. Not too many words at that. It's a living and a good one. But most of the time I don't really feel like a reporter. I feel like a party girl taking photos (pretty ones) and notes.

"Nicole!" The sound of my name in that particular tone made me sit up straighter at my desk. Even at some distance, I recognized Erica West's authoritative and well-modulated voice. It spoke of Ivy League schools and summers in France and a confident woman who was used to getting what she wanted. You could hear that right away. I didn't know what she wanted right now, but I was ready to give it to her.

Erica West is the sales manager at the *Vancouver Post*. And she is the publisher's fiancée. The over-sized diamond on her left hand tells *that* story. But neither of those things—or the ring—explained why she was in my cubicle. For the most part, our paths didn't have much reason to cross.

"Yes, Erica," I called back. "I'm right here. At my desk."

"Your desk." She sniffed when she came into the area. She wrinkled her nose just a bit as she got to my cubicle, like she might be smelling something disagreeable. There was no bad smell. Unless downsizing has an odor. There had been a lot of layoffs recently to shore up the bottom line. Not so long ago, there was a reporter in each of the ten cubicles between where Erica had entered the room and where she stood now. There were only two or three of us now.

It's a tough time for newspapers. Facebook, YouTube and millions of "citizen journalists" with their blogs and Snapchats and Instagram feeds. It all eats into everyone's news-reading time. Never mind television and radio. All of those things make people feel informed. Maybe they are and maybe they are not, but the fact is, not too many people actually read newspapers anymore. In my line of work, it seems someone talks about that—the state of the business and where we'll all be in ten years—every single day.

So Erica's desire to talk scared me. On the one hand, I was not passionate about my beat. On the other, it was a job. And a good union one at that. I am the child of immigrants. My Scottish upbringing couldn't help but make me realize that a good union job has value.

"Have a seat, Erica," I said, indicating the simple canvas chair near my desk. No one ever sits in it but my brother, Kyle. And only when he comes to get me for lunch and finds me on the phone.

She looked from the chair to me and then back at the chair, eyebrows raised. Like the very idea of sitting there startled her. She didn't answer me, nor did she take the chair, opting instead to perch on the corner of my desk. It was a maneuver that would have looked awkward had I done it. But she managed it with the elegance of a movie star, one long, silk-clad leg crossed over the other, as if the whole thing were a photo shoot.

"I'm fine," she said. "I think I'll stand."
I didn't point out that she already was not.

"You wanted to speak with me?" I
prompted.

"Did I?" She looked amused. I didn't say
anything. "Oh, well, I guess I did," she said,
examining the tips of her flawless nails.

I prepared myself for the worst, not
even sure what the worst might be.

She began without preamble on the
topic I'd expected. I could feel my heart
sinking at her words.

"As you know, we've been making
certain…cutbacks."

I didn't say anything. Just looked at
her. Of course I knew. Everyone knew. We
could barely talk about anything else. And
those of us still left at the paper walked
around the emptier spaces in a kind of
hush, waiting for something terrible to
happen.

And now? It seemed like, for me, here it was. I had a flash of me working at a Denny's. Pancake-and-sausage-filled plates balanced precariously in my arms. My hair sticking out madly from beneath a cap and streaks of sweat running down my forehead, fortunately hiding the tears.

Erica was speaking. I forced myself back from my vision to hear her words.

"In fact, we've made enough of them now. Cutbacks. We're closing off this whole floor."

So that was it, then. I had no words. I wasn't trained to be anything other than a reporter.

"When?" I managed to squeak out. My throat felt dry, as if I hadn't spoken in a long time.

"Hmmmmm?"

"How long do I have?"

"Have for what, dear girl?" The words

sounded affectionate, but I knew the tone. Erica was irritated.

"You know. Before I'm...out." I had a vision of her calling security. Having me escorted out of the building, my personal stuff in a box in my arms, with a *Don't let the door hit you on the way out.*

To my surprise, she put her head back and laughed. I knew that if she could have seen herself, she would never have done it again. The laughter changed her features. She went from composed and elegant—beautiful, really—to witch-ugly in a heartbeat.

"Oh, charming girl," she said when her laughter had run out. "You think you're fired. How very sweet."

Now I was the one who was feeling irritated. "You mean I'm not?"

"No. Definitely not. For one thing, if you were being fired, there'd be someone here from HR. Not me. And maybe some sort of counselor. We're doing that now, you know. To help with the loss."

She looked at me like she expected something, and so I said, "Oh."

"No. It's me here because this isn't a matter for HR, really. Or not exactly. It's coming from the executive suite. And no one else likes dealing with this stuff. And I don't mind. Anyway, enough of that. All that really matters is that we're going to need to buy you a desk."

"Sorry?"

She looked at me for a moment with both eyebrows fully raised. I got the feeling she couldn't quite understand how smart I was not. And then she explained my professional future to me, slowly and carefully, as if she were speaking to a child. Then I understood quite quickly. It was a chain of events I'd seen happening in the office plenty over the last few months. Too much, in fact.

I was being downsized. That was the long and the short of it. Though not severely. I wasn't being cut out or cut back, but my desk was. Or, rather, the space it was taking. I'd still have a job, was how Erica explained it. My mail would still come to the newspaper for me to pick up there. When I needed to take a meeting in an office environment, I could still do it at the newspaper. But the rest of it, I was going to have to do from home.

TWO

I decided not to think about it right away. I couldn't. I had work to do. And another party to go to. Not a party for me. I wouldn't even be part of the festivities. I'd be invisible. That's my job, what I'm paid for. And when I'm doing it right, hardly anyone even notices me.

I am a society columnist. I write about product launches. I write about fundraisers. The occasional wedding. Book launches, gallery openings, fashion shows. Really, wherever the rich and beautiful might be found in the greatest abundance, that's where I'll be.

I write about them. I take pictures. In the morning they read about themselves. The more influential among them support the paper—tell their companies to buy ads, tell their friends how great we are, because look what good taste we had in including *them*. That is the function of the society column, full stop. My column serves no purpose beyond public relations. Not really. And honestly, for this job the bar is pretty low.

I stopped at home. Changed. A pretty dress. High heels. My evening bag, which is a tiny clutch. But there was a pretty serious digital camera slung over my shoulder. An SLR. Always ready for me to pull forward at a moment's notice to grab the shot I want.

Yeah sure, I could use my smartphone for taking pictures. My competitors all do. But I want to be the best at my job. The best in the whole country if I can. And why? Because this job is not enough. If I can be the very best, I hope I will move forward.

I will move to another job at this same paper. Or at a different paper. But I'll get to be a *real* reporter. And the pictures I take will matter more than they do now. Quite a bit more.

Lately I've been using a short lens with a fixed focal length. When I throw it wide open, it's at f/1.4, which means that in normal light, only the teensiest bit of an image is in focus. Everything beyond the focus point looks soft and somewhat dreamy. It's a creative choice not everyone would make. But imagine this. You open your morning paper, check the society column, and those beautiful people? They seem even more beautiful. The photos of them are artful—that's what I'm going for. Good enough isn't good enough. I want everything I do to be extraordinary. It has to be. It's a high-water line, and I don't hit it every time. But I think I have to try.

I don't kid myself—my column isn't news. But I have a job in an industry that is dying. That makes me one of the lucky ones. It also makes me one of the ambitious ones. They don't always cancel each other out. Even so, not everything is about ambition. Things can sometimes be very simple. There are times when I am laser-focused on being the best that I can be. At other times, my needs are pretty basic. So it wasn't long before I was on a different mission, thanks to Erica's news. I knew I had only a limited amount of time to find a desk for what was to become my home office.

I'm lucky in another way too. I have a place to put a desk. Not everyone does. My apartment is in a nice part of the city. It is beyond what I could actually afford in this city, but I inherited it from a loving grandmother with both money and foresight.

As she got older and began to suspect the way my life would go, she thought I was the one of her grandkids who could use her apartment. Rather than the cash she was planning to leave the others. After all, I was a girl. And I showed every sign of not spending the energy she thought I should in looking for a husband. She despaired of me ever making anything of myself. And she thought that at some point I'd need a place to hang my hat. It's not a big apartment. But then, I don't have a lot of hats.

The apartment is on the west side of Vancouver, just a few minutes from the offices of the *Vancouver Post* by car. A few more minutes by bike and a good hour if I put rubber soles to pavement and walk. Though now that I no longer had a reason to go there every day, I was planning on doing that less often.

The apartment is bright and sunny, though small by anyone's standards. In truth, there isn't much room for new office furniture. Also, the apartment is pretty retro by virtue of having been decorated by my grandmother many years ago. So I needed a desk that would fit the decor. Not so old that was it was actually antique, but old enough to be cool. And since the newspaper had given me some money for the purpose of outfitting my office, I decided to take a good look around and get exactly the right desk. I wanted it to fit in but be functional for me as well. And for once, I wouldn't even think about the cost. I wanted something really special.

So I checked the usual places for people in my age group, but I decided I didn't want a desk that arrived home flat and in a box. There were a number of very cool stores specializing in midcentury-type furniture. But I decided retro and new would make everything else in the apartment look shabby. I couldn't afford to redecorate the whole place just because I needed a desk. Then I thought of buying something used, and I started checking auction catalogs.

It didn't take long before I found something that seemed perfect.

The desk I settled on was Danish modern. The catalog said it had been owned by Morrison Brine, a well-known Vancouver architect who had recently passed away. I liked the desk's smooth golden lines. And I liked the fact that it was a piece of furniture with some history. Best of all for me, it was exactly the size I needed. It would fit into the small available space between where I prepared my food—the kitchen—and where I sometimes consumed it—the dining area.

Not only was the desk the right size. By some strange coincidence, the auction estimate was for exactly the funds I had available—eight hundred dollars. Which was a lot for me to spend on a desk. It would take all of the money the paper had given me for outfitting my home office and a few hundred of my own loot on top. Even so, I wanted it and I set out to have it.

And I know a little bit about the way auction estimates can go. Quite often, auction items don't meet their estimates. And the desk wasn't in perfect condition. I went to the auction house to inspect it. There were a few scratches and some imperfections in the varnish, as well as some scars where someone had tried to open a locked drawer. I knew the scratches would be under my laptop when I was working on it, so what did I care? And there again, that perfect size. I'd brought a tape measure to be sure. I measured the desk again to confirm that it was just right. It seemed to me that it was meant to be my desk.

On the day of the auction, I took my seat at the back of the room and settled in to acquire my desk. This would be the first time I'd ever tried to buy anything at auction. I couldn't believe how excited I was.

I had to sit through a lot of other things before they got to my desk. I didn't have to sit there for the whole day though. It wasn't one of the big-ticket items they were holding until the end.

I sat there on my hands and just watched. I sat on my hands. We've all seen auctions on television where someone scratches their nose and ends up spending half a million bucks on a vase. I didn't have half a million bucks kicking around for a vase or anything else, so I thought I'd better not scratch my nose. Of course, as soon as I had that thought, my nose got incredibly itchy.

So I sat there. On my hands. And waited for what seemed like an endless number of items to get sold. Although I have to acknowledge that it seemed like an even longer time because my nose got itchier and itchier.

But the watching was interesting. An ancient Incan vase went for practically nothing. It didn't make sense to me that a vase more than three thousand years old would fetch so much less than the really ugly one that followed it. That one was made in the late twentieth century and looked like something from a garage sale. Then another vase, this time from ancient Peru. Three hundred and fifty bucks. I had to hold my hand down so I didn't bid. It seemed like a really good deal. So very old. So crudely beautiful. But I didn't raise my hand. I needed all my loot in case the desk went for a higher-than-expected price. I wanted the desk that badly.

On and on the auction went. And then, finally, it was time for lot 164. I sat up straighter.

The auctioneer described the desk as a piece of midcentury Danish modern furniture designed "in the style of Grete Jalk." This didn't mean anything to me, but I took it to mean that though the desk was not quite a museum piece, it was close.

I started to get worried. If the desk was a collector piece, it could go for a lot more than the estimate. I sat tight and hung on.

According to the auctioneer, good old Morrison Brine had sat at the desk for all of its years. Plotting or phoning or doodling. Probably not designing, as it wasn't big enough for that. But it was a desk that had often been at the center of inspiration. I liked the feeling of that.

Sitting at the back of the room, I'd been looking the crowd over since I got there. The whole time, I'd been trying to figure out who looked like a collector who might end up competing with me for the desk, and who looked like a regular desk buyer. The person who put the first bid on my desk was not one of the people I would have marked as competition.

He did not look like a collector at all. Not to me anyway. I could tell he was tall even though he was sitting down—something about the distance between his shoulders and where his butt nestled against the chair. I had a sense that when he stood up he'd be over six feet tall. He had dark hair falling over his bronze forehead in a way that kept drawing my eye. I remembered those details not only because he was a remarkably handsome man, but because there was something familiar about him. I couldn't quite place him, but I kept looking at him and wondering.

He started the bidding at two hundred dollars. I bid two fifty. He bid two seventy-five. I went right to three. We went on in that fashion for a couple more rounds, until he bid right up to eight hundred, the estimated price. Then he turned around and looked back at me. He didn't seem like someone who'd let a little thing like money stop him. So I threw in what I figured would be my last bid, eight fifty. It was over my budget, but I knew it didn't matter anyway. I could have bid a thousand and he would still have gone higher. As I placed my bid, I resigned myself to a life with a less interesting, still-to-be-discovered desk and sighed.

I could see he was about to make what would likely have been the last bid, but he never got the chance. The auction room's doors burst open and half a dozen uniformed Vancouver city policemen stomped in. Everything stopped. The auctioneer stood poised with his gavel in midair. They descended on Tall, Dark and Handsome.

I saw him see the cops. See that they were there for him. He half-rose. I thought he might make a run for it, but there was nowhere to go. All of the assembled auction-goers watched in astonishment as the guy was quickly arrested and cuffed. The officers read him his rights, then frog-marched him out the door. His dark hair kept falling over his forehead and flopping helplessly, because his hands weren't free to push it back.

It all happened so quickly that once he was gone, we all just stood and looked around the room and at each other. Had that really happened, we all seemed to wonder, or were we imagining things?

The auction didn't go back to normal as soon as the cops left. A murmur flowed through the crowd. No one knew quite what to do.

Once the auction started up again, the auctioneer announced that the sale of the item that had been on the block at the time of the "disturbance" would be restarted from the beginning. And that's what happened.

When the hammer fell after the sale, the desk was mine for $575. I was pleased but also astonished. And I smiled to myself. Fate had intended the desk to be mine. Another few minutes and the tall guy would have owned the desk *and* been carted away to jail. I'd caught a lucky break.

My new desk. I went and looked at it again. On closer inspection and now that the deed was done, I could see it was not in quite as good a condition as I had thought. Most irritating of all, the largest drawer was locked. And it did not seem to have a key. I hoped that when I paid for the desk, the key would turn up through the auction office. But I had a feeling it would not. Partly because, as I'd noticed before, the smooth and elegant lock that held the drawer shut appeared to have been jimmied at some point. Some of the scratches were due to that.

I wanted to pay for the desk and get it home, but based on the events in the auction room, I had an important call to make first. I was pleased with myself for realizing that. Maybe I had what it took to be a reporter after all.

"Webb!" The editor of the *Vancouver Post* had a deep male voice. He shouted his last name as he answered. One of his habits and a nod back to a time when city editors barked first and asked questions later. Mike Webb was from the old school.

"Hey, Mike. It's Nicole. I think I just caught a story."

"No kidding. What have you got?" There was caution in his voice. I understood. I was not one of his reporters. Strictly speaking, the city editor was not my boss, but he *was* the boss of all the news. On the editorial side, nothing got into the paper without his okay. And he and I both knew I didn't want to be a gossip columnist forever. I wanted to do hard news. And Mike wasn't against me doing it, but, as I'd seen very recently, budgets were being cut. That meant fewer pages, which meant less room for news. And *that* ultimately meant that every item we ran had double freight. Space in the paper was precious, and Mike had reporters to fill the paper with stories he had assigned them. I could hear it in his voice—the last thing he needed was me sailing in there and messing with his system.

"I'm at Lively Auctions. Personal business on my own time." Which was mostly true. "I was bidding on a piece of furniture. Suddenly cops burst in, grab a guy and take him away."

"And no one is dead this time?"

I grinned despite myself. "No, Mike. Everyone is alive."

"Okay, good. Murder is definitely above your pay grade."

"Thanks," I said. "I'll keep that in mind."

"Good. But anyway, sure. Look into this one. What harm could it do?"

I tried not to bristle at his patronizing tone. He was city editor, and he was not a chatty guy. If I wanted warm and fuzzy,

I'd have to go somewhere else. A puppy maybe. Mike Webb was never going to supply it.

In the office at the auction house, before I paid, I asked about the arrest. No one knew any more than I did. But I discovered I had an even bigger challenge. There was a problem with my credit card.

"But that's impossible," I told the clerk. "I know I have funds available."

The girl behind the counter looked at me with flat eyes. She'd heard this one before.

"Sorry," she said, but she didn't seem sorry. "I can't help you with that, hon. You'll have to call the company or whatever. But the item doesn't leave here without payment."

Since I didn't want to make a trip back, I called my mom and made arrangements for her to pay for the desk over the phone. I'd pick up cash to repay her when I stopped at the bank to see what was wrong with my card.

Then it was just a matter of getting the desk home. Luckily for me, three nice men wrangled it into the back of my car. The piece was way heavier than it looked, they said. I thought that was funny in a way. The classic midcentury lines looked light, maybe even insignificant, to the untrained eye. But the guys who moved the desk to my car heaved and shoved as they muscled it around. Was teak heavy? I wondered. I told myself I'd look that up.

With the desk carefully nestled into the packing materials they supplied, I drove off, my new prize sticking out of the hatch of my car.

At the other end I had arranged for Kyle to be there to help me. Considering the weight of the beast, we enlisted one of my neighbors to help get it upstairs. But it was Kyle who ensured it made the journey safely, avoiding the corners on the stairs and handling the desk with the care one gives a long-lost child.

The three of us positioned it exactly where I had envisioned. And it was perfect. It looked just right in the sunny light that floods my apartment. I was so happy.

"Good choice," Kyle said approvingly when my neighbor was gone. "It will be a nice, bright place for you to work."

"I think so," I agreed. "There's one more thing I need your help with though."

I showed him the locked desk drawer, and he went to work. He got out a credit card and a screwdriver and did a couple of things to try to open it, but the lock didn't budge.

"Sorry, Nic. I'm sure I can get it open, but I'll have to come back with some real tools."

We agreed he'd come by the following day to try to open the desk. Once he was gone I got around to the business of thinking about what my evening was going to look like.

It was Tuesday. Early in the week, but it looked to be an interesting night. There was a book launch at a wine bar out near the university and a gallery opening in the downtown core. I expected both events would be well attended and the food would probably be good.

Of the two, the one I really *had* to attend was the book launch. The book in question had been written by one of the *Post*'s reporters. Which meant there was an expectation that the paper would cover the event. After all, he was one of our own. How the book did would reflect on the paper.

The author was the paper's wine guy, and the book was called *1,001 BC Wines*. The title surprised me, as I wouldn't have imagined there were that many, but it did mean that the snacks would be good. In my experience, wine and snacks tend to appear together at such events. I redoubled my efforts to arrive on time. I didn't want to get there after the food had run out.

I arrived a little after seven to a surprisingly small turnout. My first clue had been the amount of parking available when I pulled up. There was lots. I parked easily and let myself into the darkened space.

As I'd expected, since the author was a colleague, I recognized some faces right away. But it's a big paper. I'd never met the author before, and his face was unfamiliar. I let him know who I was and we chatted easily for a bit. There wasn't a big crowd, so it wasn't like we had to shout above the din. He was an affable guy. His name was Clark Biederman, and he looked as you'd expect a wine writer to look. He was jowly and pleasant. But he didn't seem to have a lot of friends, though he looked like a guy who would have many. Few of them had attended anyway. Maybe he'd been flogging his book for a while and his friends were avoiding him.

Like mine, Clark's job was one of those that had been moved right out of the office. So although both of us were full-time employees of the paper, neither of us actually worked there anymore.

Clark kept thanking me for coming and kept trying to top up my glass. And since it was very good wine, it was hard for me to resist. I did, though, because it was only my first stop. There was still a whole lot of evening to get through.

I was working. I positioned Clark in such a way that the four or six friends who had attended looked more like a backdrop of fans. Then I took a bunch of photos.

"Are you working on a book, Nicole?" Clark asked me at one point. I told him I wasn't.

"You should think about it. It's the one thing that makes you an expert in your field."

I thought about that as I drove to my next event. In what field would I even want to be recognized as an expert? Choosing which invitations are most likely to produce the best food and drink? If I was ever going to write a book, I'd need to find something I was passionate about *and* also good at. I didn't even know where to start.

The gallery opening proved more lively. There were three featured artists. They were young and their work was vibrant, as was the crowd. No wine this time, just funky flavors from a local nano-brewery. And since it was one I'd never heard of before, I figured one of the bearded hipster friends of the artists was probably the brewmaster.

I took photos of each of the artists in front of one of their own large canvases. While I did that, I knew my column for the next day was pretty much writing itself. The paintings would look great reproduced in color, which I knew the paper would do. The artists' faces were eager and beautiful. And in his own way, Clark and his book and little crowd had proven to be colorful. With the rows of bottles and glasses, Clark's happy face and his elbow patches, those pictures would be fun too.

I went home to write my column, the first time I'd truly worked in my new home-office space. And the work went easily and well. A promising start. The photos along with a few well-chosen words were easily filed, fulfilling my professional duties for another day.

A good day, all in all. And full. It was possible in that moment to think my home-based work life would be peaceful. Calm.

THREE

My brother came by the next day around noon. I buzzed him in and he trudged upstairs, toolbox in hand.

"Don't know what we might find in that desk, eh?" He winked as he took up his tools and settled in to work.

"Thanks, Kyle," I said. "I'll make us some tea."

While I boiled water, I realized I had a knot of excitement in my stomach. And the excitement had nothing to do with tea and everything to do with what might be in that desk. And, of course, it might be nothing.

But a locked drawer…it seemed to me to imply possibilities. After all, why lock a drawer if there is nothing inside?

My mind went through options. I discarded them one by one. But I was confident that whatever happened, there was something to be found. Call it a hunch.

As I walked toward Kyle with the tray, the locked drawer sprang open.

I put the tea things down and we both stood there, staring at rich wood grain and careful joinery.

It was empty. The drawer held nothing at all.

"But that doesn't make any sense," I said. "Who locks an empty drawer?"

"No one, that's who," Kyle said.

I poured us both a cup of tea while he moved back and forth, looking here and there. He tugged at the top of the desk in a way that indicated he thought it might move. It didn't. Then he swung down onto his knees and peered up and under. Nothing again. It was pointless, I thought. There was nothing there. But he was so intent on what he was doing, I didn't have the heart to discourage him.

At a certain point, Kyle went back to looking at the desk, the empty drawer pulled open like a gaping mouth.

I didn't see anything to keep looking at and was about to go and do something else when I felt more than saw Kyle come to attention.

"What the…" he muttered.

"What is it? What do you see?"

He didn't answer, instead focusing on whatever it was I could not see.

He paced one way, then the other, peering at the desk from all angles. Then he moved back again. Pushed the drawer in. Pulled it out. Pushed it back in. Stuck his arm way in with the drawer partly open. Moved around back again, knocking against the wood. Suddenly I felt as much as saw Kyle's energy change.

"What?" I said. And when he kept ignoring me, I got more insistent. "*What?*"

"There's something in there, Nic."

I shook my head. "I don't think so. I mean, look." I pointed at the desk. "It's empty."

"Not in the drawer. I think there's a chamber behind the drawer."

"A chamber?" I imagined a vast room. I knew that couldn't be what he meant, but I couldn't get the picture out of my head.

"Yeah." He pulled the drawer open again. Reached inside. "See? This area is larger than what we're seeing. Bottom and back."

"Are you saying there's a false back?"

But he didn't answer. Instead, with a determined look on his face, he pulled a small crowbar out of his toolbox and moved in the direction of the desk.

"Hey!" I said when it looked like he was about to resort to force.

"If I'm right, what I'm about to break through wasn't part of the desk in the first place."

"Whatever. I paid a week's salary for that desk!" At that moment, it didn't seem relevant that it had been mostly the newspaper's money, not mine.

He seemed not to have heard me, and it wasn't long before I heard a loud crack followed by the splintering of wood.

"Holy Dinah!" It came from Kyle, but it could just as easily have been me. He looked up, eyes wide, from where he crouched on the floor in front of the desk. He'd been right. With a few quick chops, he'd broken through what he'd correctly guessed was the false back of the drawer. And there was something inside.

I watched Kyle, down on his knees, reach in and feel around. After a while his hand came back out. In it was what looked at first to be an oblong bundle of paper.

He laid it on the floor and looked at me questioningly.

I shrugged. "Yeah, I guess. Go ahead."

Cautiously, he pulled away layer upon layer of protective paper.

When all the paper was out of the way, we saw that the wrapping had been protecting a wine bottle unlike any I'd ever seen. The glass was thick and dark, with letters embossed on it. The label was slightly yellowed but otherwise perfect. Kyle reached inside the drawer again and pulled out another bundle. And then another after that. In all, he brought out half a dozen bottles, which he unwrapped and lined up on the surface of the desk. Quite a pile of old paper was left behind. I gathered it all up and shoved it into the desk. I thought we'd deal with it when the time came to repair the hole my brother had made discovering the hidden chamber.

"*Concordia Monastery,*" Kyle read aloud. "*Very fine wine. Kelowna, British Columbia.* You ever heard of them?"

I shook my head.

"Me neither. What do we do?" he said. We looked at each other without blinking. A family trait in times of pressure, that not-blinking thing.

"Drink it?" I said.

He gave me a long look. Then we both looked at the tea and back at each other.

"I'll go get glasses," I said. Because drinking it seemed as good a place to start as any.

As I was returning from the kitchen with the wineglasses, my phone rang. And before the ring had settled into our ears, Kyle's phone went off as well. Our eyes met as we picked up. My mother was calling me. And Kyle? I could see right away that he was talking to Dad.

I tried to focus on the voice. It was near hysteria, unusual for my mom.

"We've had a break-in, lass. Imagine!"

"You're all right?"

"Och, aye. We weren't here. Your da was at the golf, of course. And I was down the way at Mary's for a cup of tea."

"It happened during the day?"

"Yes. That's what I'm saying. They broke in bold as anything in broad middle of the day. Just now. Imagine!"

"What did they take?"

"Well, that's the thing, isn't it? They made a big mess, but nothing seems to be missing."

"Nothing at all?"

"That's right. The place was ransacked. But nothing as we can see is gone."

"That doesn't make any sense."

"Aye. That's what we thought as well. And it's not like we're drug dealers or anything. Just simple people. We've nothing to hide."

There was more along these lines. I felt the unfamiliar shiver of concern for my parents that must be akin to the feelings parents always have for their kids. I couldn't bear the thought of something happening to them and hated that they were having to deal with something frightening that was out of my control.

When I hung up, my brother was already off the phone. He was sitting there looking at me, concern raw on his face.

"It was Dad. He was very upset."

"Mom too. I've got some time this afternoon. I'm going to drive up there and see if I can reassure them."

"I'll come with you," Kyle said.

We drove out to Burnaby in my brother's Volvo convertible. It's a crazy car for an out-of-work artist, but he's always liked nice things, and he'd married a woman who could afford to give them to him. For a while. The marriage had been over for years, but some of the residuals lived on. He'd kept the car. He'd gotten the cat. I didn't judge. And ever since the relationship ended, he was always available to help me if I got in a jam.

When we pulled up, Kyle and I could see that our parents' home on Capitol Hill was teeming with activity. The driveway and the curb at the front of the house were lined with cars neither of us recognized. We exchanged a glance as we drove past. Kyle parked farther up the block, and we walked back.

When we opened the front door we found the house flooded with the kind of noise that can only be properly made by Scots. A bunch of them.

"Och, no, you don't say."

"Aye, Gladys, that's right. Ye can't imagine."

And so on, a story being told and retold. And maybe it was growing in the telling. Changing shape. Kyle and I could only guess.

"What the hell, Mom?" I said when I cornered her in the bedroom, separated for the moment from her gaggles of concerned friends. "You were never in any danger, right?"

"Well, you don't really know sich a thing, do you? He coulda still been in the house when we got back. The possibility seemed distinct."

Distinct. "Ah," I said. "And did that prove to be the case?"

"Well, no. I came home to this." She indicated the bedroom we stood in. A half-stripped bed, dresser drawers open, waste-paper baskets overturned. "This is not the way I left things."

I just looked at her. I didn't doubt her words for a heartbeat. I could not imagine a situation where Mom would leave the house with the bed unmade, let alone things strewn on the floor.

"Do you have any idea who it might have been?"

"Oh no, lass. Not at all. You know, we've never had such a thing happen."

"And you say nothing is missing?"

"Not so's we've been able to tell, at any rate. It doesn't appear to be. But Marjorie MacDougall said when she was broken into last year, it took her and Hamish a whole month to realize the extent of what was gone. They took her *eyeglasses*, if you kin imagine. And the wee change purse she'd kept after her mother went on, poor soul."

I resisted the urge to travel with her through the recollection of Marjorie's break-in. "So far nothing though, right?"

"Aye."

"And certainly, if there was danger before, it's now passed."

We settled them down as well as we could. Large amounts of tea were consumed. We ate a bunch of biscuits. After a while Mom and Dad seemed to calm, and Kyle said he had to go because he had a thing. I asked him to drop me at the office on his way. My parents stood in the driveway, waving goodbye as we left. They suddenly seemed so small and vulnerable to me. I felt a wave of something indefinable and unfamiliar wash over me. It was love, sure, but something else too. Something that tasted a bit like fear.

FOUR

The offices of the *Vancouver Post* are big and impressive. An office tower near the ocean in the financial district. I'm used to it now. I hardly think about it when I'm coming and going, but the first time I came through the big front doors, I had to hide the shake of my hand and try to ignore the butterflies in my stomach. It was all so big and impressive. And me? I was naive. And so green, I thought that as a journalist I would bring evil to light and change the world.

I'd been one of the top students in my graduating class. My grades had been quite good, and I guess I'd shown promise. I'd landed one of the half dozen intern spots available at various media outlets in the area. In the natural course of things, that might have helped me get a job after graduation. But something happened that gave my career a shove instead of a push. The guy who had been doing the paper's society beat for thirty years died. Nothing mysterious or even especially out of the ordinary. He just wore out. But there had been no warning—he just keeled over in the middle of a week when a lot of important events were happening that needed covering.

So there was me, beavering away in the homes section during my internship. Writing reviews of new condo developments. Rewriting press releases about the latest high-tech kitchen taps and the newest laundry-room technology. In the middle of that, someone from the city desk had put his head through my doorway.

"You know how to use a digital camera?"

I'd looked at him and let him look back at me. Based on my age and gender, was there any possibility I did not?

"I do," I'd said finally.

"You have any problems with going to parties alone?"

This had seemed a potentially loaded question, so I'd tried to think fast before I answered. I couldn't see the end game, though, so I'd answered honestly.

"I do not."

"Okay, great," he'd said, looking relieved. "There's a fashion show at Turmeric 95 tonight." I knew the nightclub. It was on Granville. I'd gotten the idea he was glad I'd said yes. That if I hadn't been up for it, he would have had to do it himself.

And that was how it had started. As easy as that. I went to the party. Took the pictures.

Identified and made nice with the key folks. Went back to the office and wrote about it.

To call what I do reporting is a stretch of anyone's imagination. But it gives me a paycheck, and not a bad one, and at least I am working in the industry I trained for. Not everyone is lucky enough to do that.

All of that said, it didn't mean I wanted to leave the building in a box in twenty-five or thirty years, the way my predecessor had. I liked my job and I didn't want to lose it, but I knew from the beginning that, as things were, it wasn't enough. Not forever anyway. And maybe not for long.

After I'd collected my mail and read through my various invitations, I went to the newsroom and plunked myself at an empty desk. I picked up the phone and dialed a direct line to the Vancouver police department. Sergeant Itani answered right away.

"Hey, Rosa," I said, "it's Nicole Charles at the *Vancouver Post*. There was an arrest at Lively Auctions yesterday. I was in the house. And it happened to be the guy I was bidding against. So truly, it could not have been better timing. I ended up getting an amazing deal on a desk."

Rosa laughed. "Oh dear. Though I guess that's good?"

"Yeah. Anyway, I thought I'd call and see if I could impose on you. I need information, and all the other ways in seem too steep. Can you find out who the guy was?"

It wasn't Rosa's job to give me information. She wasn't a communications officer. But we'd met a few months earlier and hit it off. I knew she'd dig to get at whatever information was available. And she knew I wouldn't ask her to go any further than she felt she could.

"Hmmmm…let me check. What day did you say it was? Yesterday? And what time?"

I told her, then heard a computer keyboard clacking.

"Yes. I see it here in the system. Your guy was arrested on suspicion."

"Suspicion of what?" I wanted to know.

"Oddly"—Rosa sounded perplexed— "that's a little unclear. I'll check and get back to you."

"Great. Can you email deets on the perp?" Yes, I realized I sounded like a reporter on a television show. I really had to quit watching late-night TV.

"The ones I can release now, sure."

I'd promised Mike a story, but I really didn't have much to write about. Yet. An arrest at an auction house. Sure, it was something. But not enough to make it into the story I needed if I had any hope of ever getting off the gossip beat.

I got Rosa's email a half hour later. It gave me enough for a small item. I knew even while I wrote it that it would get buried deep in the first section, but I didn't have a choice.

AUCTION-HOUSE ARREST
INVITES QUESTIONS

A mysterious arrest at Lively Auctions in North Burnaby on Monday inter-rupted the sale and left attendees wondering what was going on.

Half a dozen uniformed officers appeared in the early afternoon and arrested Joseph MacLeish (28) of Vancouver on suspicion of criminal activity. Vancouver City Police would not release further information in what is an ongoing investigation.

The disturbance unsettled an auction in progress. The sale continued once MacLeish was been taken into custody and removed from the premises.

It was an insignificant item that contained almost no information, but it was the best I could do with what was available. I'd have to hope I found more to add for the next day's edition.

With the first story written and filed, I thought I'd try to get a little more information on what I'd found in my desk. It occurred to me that Clark Biederman, wine expert, author and colleague, might have some answers. If not about the wine itself, at least where it had most recently come from.

I checked the company directory for Clark Biederman's direct line. Voice mail greeted me when I dialed it.

"Clark, this is Nicole Charles. Fun hanging with you last night, and all the best with your book! I have some questions on an unrelated topic. Please call me when you get a chance."

After I hung up, I thought about what I knew. Admittedly, not much, though I felt

I was close to seeing something right in front of me.

For lack of any better ideas, I typed "Morrison Brine" into a search engine. As I already knew, Brine had been a key player in the development of mid-twentieth-century Vancouver. He had died at age eighty-nine—no spring chicken—and in his younger years there had been shadows. Nothing was said outright, of course. Not in newspaper stories. But it seemed to me there were things between the lines. I made a note to delve further.

His career had been above reproach. He was best known for an office tower in Taipei in the 1980s. Although some of the designs he had made in Vancouver rivaled that building for sheer stature and innovation.

Beyond all of this, what caught my eye was a photo. Morrison Brine in the 1970s, looking strong, handsome and oddly familiar.

I was sure I'd never met the man, but there was something in this photo that made me think again.

I wanted to see more photos, so I did an image search and got some satisfying results. It seemed that from early on in his career, Brine had been a star in his field. There had been many awards, many opening days, many splendid events…and many photos. In all of them, I saw the same thing. He was handsome, distinguished-looking…and very familiar-looking to me.

While all of this was interesting, it didn't take long for me to realize that this particular line of research wasn't moving me ahead. With my first story completed on deadline, it was time to see if I could find anything more on Joseph MacLeish. But it's a big world. And I knew better than most that there are a lot of people with Scottish names in it.

So I tried a new search: "Joseph+ MacLeish+Vancouver." And a whole lot of things I knew to be unrelated to my search came up. Dead old guys. Sports heroes. Entertainment personalities.

Buried deep on the fourth page of results, I found a link to a notice of a stock splitting, and when I followed it, a photo opened, almost large as life. The remnants of my Morrison Brine searches were still on the monitor, and MacLeish's picture opened right next to one of Brine. And I felt my breath catch. With MacLeish onscreen next to the Morrison Brine of thirty years ago, the two could have been brothers. There was so much that was similar about them. The cut of the chin. The cast of the eyes. I had seen that Brine was a tall man, and I already knew that MacLeish was too.

Looking at them side by side, it seemed obvious to me. And the timing was right:

the two men were a generation apart. But it was too much of a coincidence for sure. Surely it would be too flukey if MacLeish was Morrison Brine's son.

FIVE

Before I had the chance to really digest any of this, my phone rang. Clark Biederman was returning my call.

"Have you ever heard of Concordia Monastery?" I asked when our greetings were complete.

"Why, yes, of course," he responded.

I waited a beat before pushing forward. "And...?"

"And...what?" he asked.

"Can you tell me about it?"

"Oh yes. I thought...well, I thought since you were asking that you knew."

"Knew what?" I asked, trying my hardest not to sound exasperated.

"About the winery."

"I. Do. Not," I replied, careful to keep my voice calm though I felt close to bursting.

"There was a winery near Kelowna called Concordia Monastery."

My eyes shot toward the ceiling. I counted the panels between the air-conditioning outflow and the wall. *One. Two. Three.*

"Yes..." I prompted.

"For a good long while, it was the top winery in the province. You will have seen it mentioned in my book."

His book. I'd forgotten all about it.

"I must have missed that part," I said quietly.

"Anyway," Clark said, sounding only slightly huffy, "it says that the Concordia Monastery has a treasured place in the history of British Columbian wines. Canadian wines, come to think of it. See, at a time when—to be frank—many wineries were making rotgut—"

"Rotgut?" I interrupted.

"As in 'rot your guts.' Very bad wine," he explained. "But Concordia was producing wines that could compete with what were then the very best wines in the world. Despite being made with fox grapes."

"Fox grapes?" It was like he was speaking a different language.

"The *Vitis labrusca* family of vines. Used widely in winemaking to this day. Fox grapes are, in fact, native to North America. Concord is one of the more well-known varieties. In Concordia Monastery's time, it was the most common variety in North America."

"And what time *would* this be?" I'd interrupted him, but it seemed important for context.

"Why, the teens, of course. Of the twentieth century—1917 or thereabouts."

"Of course," I murmured, and he went on.

"Concord grapes are hardy and do well in many climates. However, they generally have a sort of foxiness about them that doesn't, in the end, lend itself to fine wine. But at Concordia, they brought that humble vine to new heights. They created a wine that was venerated throughout the viticulture of the time."

I raised my eyebrows at his use of lofty words but didn't remark on it. Everyone liked the wine, is what he was saying. I got it. Maybe they even liked it a lot.

"And it was all made by the monks?"

"No, not at all. See, that was one of the remarkable things. There was no actual monastery at Concordia Monastery."

"Pardon? That doesn't make sense. Why put the word *Monastery* right on the bottle if there wasn't one?"

He laughed, and I could tell he was pleased to share his knowledge. "At the time, only religious orders could get the licensing required to make wine. As I said, this was at the time of Prohibition."

"I thought that was only in the United States."

"Mostly. In British Columbia, Prohibition was enacted in 1917. It only lasted just into the 1920s. But that was the period in which Concordia got going. By the time the ban was repealed, Concordia Monastery was the moniker, and they kept it. But Concordia had no actual religious affiliation. Even the name was kind of an inside joke. Concordia as in Concord grape, nothing to do with the Roman goddess of harmony or the university or any other Concordia at all."

"Is the winery still around in some form?"

"Well, after all that, you'd think so, wouldn't you? But no. Though that's what I find so intriguing."

"What's that?"

"Well, the wine, you see. It was so superior, it was remarkable." He laughed. "Remarkable! So remarkable, in fact, it was remarked upon around the globe."

I got the point. *Remarkable*. He'd said it three times. The wine was really good.

"Concordia Monastery's 1929 vintage was particularly superior and won them accolades in France, where it was exhibited. Early in 1930, though, the winery shut down under mysterious circumstances. But that '29 Concordia, which was what they called it, became legendary. In fact, it became something of a holy grail."

"How so?"

"As a rule, British Columbian wines are not collectible. Even today. There are some obvious exceptions, of course. But for the most part, no. But the Concordias of that era truly are. Everything about them contributed to this. The unique way they were bottled. The fineness of the wine itself. The mystery that came via the demise of the winery. All of it."

"So it's collectible. What do you think that might mean?

"Pardon?"

"Put a value on it."

"Hard to say, really. But at auction a few years ago, a case of the '28 went for half a million dollars."

"*What?*" I didn't know a lot about wine, but that seemed like a lot to me.

"That's right. The '29 might very well be priceless."

He told me more, but I didn't hear a lot of it. *Priceless*. I wanted to get off the phone. I wanted to get home.

I couldn't get to my car fast enough. Once I was driving, it seemed that traffic had never been so slow. I parked hurriedly and raced up the stairs, slowing only when I couldn't get my key into the lock.

And when I finally did and the door opened, there, of course, it was.

The bottles I had were all labeled *1929*.

SIX

It appeared Kyle and I had almost opened and drunk a priceless bottle of wine. The very thought made me swoon.

The kind of money Biederman had talked about was not chump change. It was the sort that can change lives. More to the point, the kind of money that people will go to great lengths to both acquire and protect. Joseph MacLeish had been bidding against me for the desk. Did he know about the wine? It seemed likely. It was time to do more digging.

When I'd seen their photographs side by side, I'd noticed the physical similarity between Morrison Brine and Joseph MacLeish. I needed to see if there was an actual connection. I decided to head to the newspaper's morgue and see if I could find evidence of one.

Of course, the paper's morgue is mostly electronic now. But I knew there was still a room where copies of the earliest editions were kept. There were also microfiche of the editions between the earliest and those of the late 1980s, when everything started to be collected digitally. In my three years on the job, I'd never needed to find the morgue before, so I had to ask where it was. When I was directed to the basement, I wasn't surprised.

Microfiche was used in the era before digitization to store information that would take up too much room in physical form. Looking at it is like looking at strips of negatives. There was a time when it was someone's job to photograph every page of every edition and put it into microfiche form. That would have been a tedious job.

I knew about microfiche from high school and my journalism studies. But I'd never had to deal with it in a real-life situation until now. The newspaper microfiche was archived by day and date so that if something needed to be looked up at some future point, it would be relatively easy to find. And I say *relatively* because nowadays, we are used to random access. We can enter a date or a name or phrase, and a computer will find what we're looking for, easy peasy. Microfiche isn't like that. No actual data has been stored —just photographs of data. You have to find the film for the date you want and then load that piece of film into a reader that looks like an old-timey computer. And then you just poke around and read until you find something. The whole process does not lend itself to a fast search.

And so I loaded and poked and prodded away, surprised when I checked the time after a while and found that several hours had passed. It was quiet down in that room. There might once have been some sort of keeper or librarian down here in the archives. There wasn't now. I'd inserted my ID card into a computer to gain entry, and that was it. Finding the history I needed was up to me.

I found myself following certain types of searches. The mention of a new building being designed by Morrison Brine would lead me forward a year or so to the dedication of the building. Or to some event celebrating it at which a photo might have been taken. It was painstaking work. Wedding notices. Birth announcements.

Announcements of marriages and engagements. Until, finally, I found what I'd been looking for. A gorgeous Vancouver day. A society event that the guy doing my job in those days would have been documenting. A good photograph from the mid-1980s. Morrison Brine, his much younger wife and their three sons. All of them fair and blue-eyed like their mother. None who could have grown to be the man who had bid against me for the desk.

I sat back, mission accomplished. But I had a hollow feeling. It was confirmed—I was back to square one. That feeling subsided as I was packing up the last of the microfiche. Something caught my eye. It was a news item from 1955, the first time Morrison Brine's name had ever been mentioned by the *Vancouver Post*. It was a small item. So small I'd gone right past it my first time through:

YOUNG ARCHITECT WINS
BIG ASSIGNMENT

Morrison Brine, a recent hire at the esteemed Vancouver firm of Matheson, Chase has been fingered to design investor Enzo Rossi's new Southwest Marine Drive estate. The aforementioned estate has been much mentioned in this newspaper over the last few years. At ten thousand square feet, it will be, upon completion, the largest private residence west of Toronto.

There was more. Describing the Italianate fixtures that were being brought in. And gold newel-posts and bathroom taps. The private ice arena *and* indoor pool that were being designed. The house still existed. It was now owned by the city and rented out for functions. I'd been to a few society events there as a reporter.

As a private residence, the place was so grand it was stupid, but it was a great venue for weddings and the like.

None of that was remarkable to me in this moment. What *was* remarkable was that Morrison Brine, then a junior designer and at the whopping age of (I did the math) twenty-eight, should be awarded such a plum of a job. It made no sense. I was not an expert on the hierarchy of architectural offices, but it only added up that they were like everything else— juniors get the crappiest gigs. You earn the good assignments. And there he was, a nobody of twenty-eight, designing some fancy house.

Before I had time to think about it very much, my phone rang. It was Rosa Itani, getting back to me as promised.

"So actually," she started without preamble, "there's not much I can tell you. Not much beyond what you already know."

"I was afraid of that," I admitted. "But since I don't know much of anything, whatever you add will give me more."

"Okay then. You have the name?"

"You sent that in email."

"Right. Joseph MacLeish. The team you saw making the arrest had been staking him out for some time."

"Staking him out. Like, following him everywhere?"

"And watching what he was doing. That's right. Our organized-crime squad has had him under observation for some time."

"Organized crime."

"Yes. Mafia, specifically."

"Mafia? That makes me think *Godfather*-type stuff. Do you mean something different?"

"Sadly, no. I do not. We have *Godfather*-style Mafia in Vancouver."

I digested that, feeling it should not have surprised me. If I wanted to be a crime reporter, I was going to have to know stuff like this.

"So what is MacLeish doing with the Mafia? What is his involvement?"

"A good question. And a fair one."

"But you can't answer it, can you?" I'd heard something in her voice.

"That's right, Nicole. Sorry. It's part of an ongoing investigation."

"Investigation of…?" I prompted.

"Nice try."

"Anything more you *can* tell me?"

I heard papers shuffling. "MacLeish is six foot three. And he weighs 190."

"O-kaay. Can I ask something else?"

"You can try."

"The arrest. Did it have anything to do with architecture? Or wine?"

That got a soft chuckle from Rosa. "Those are about as different from each other as I can imagine, and…no. Both counts. I can honestly say, based on what

I know, that it had nothing to do with either of those things."

I sighed. "It was worth a shot."

"You sound pathetic." Rosa laughed. "So what the hell? I'll throw you a bone. MacLeish had been promoting a stock."

"What does that mean?"

"It means he was pumping it around town—you know, talking it up, trying to get people to buy it so the price would go up."

"Is that legal?"

"Within limits, yes."

"And he exceeded those limits?"

"That I can't tell you. But I'll say this—we still have him. I guess you knew that. He's in remand, awaiting a court appearance."

"Wait. You said he's in remand. What's he charged with?"

"False stock promotion, but between you and me, it's not going to stick. They wanted to hold him. It's not him they're after so much. It's the bad boys he's been running around with."

"And the suspicion was that the stock had a Mafia tie-in?" She hesitated, so I answered for her. "You can't tell me that either, can you?"

Another chuckle. "Can't pull one over on you, Nicole."

"But you said it's not going to stick, so maybe no Mafia connection."

"Maybe," she said cagily. "But closer than wine. Or architects."

"Great," I said. Another dead end. We said goodbye and hung up, but then I had a different thought and called her right back.

"Sorry, Rosa. Me again. You said Mafia. But that's just a word we use, isn't it? An expression."

"How do you mean?"

"Well, Mafia is sort of a catchphrase for organized crime, isn't it? We've all heard it—Russian Mafia or Gay Mafia or whatever. That's what you mean, right? When you say Mafia. Organized crime."

"Well, I get what you're saying. That *can* be the case. But it isn't here. That's why I didn't qualify it. I didn't say the some-thing Mafia because I meant it in the classic sense. The Cosa Nostra."

"Italian." It was little more than a whisper from me as pieces started to fall into place.

"Sicilian," Rosa corrected. "And yes, there has traditionally been a strong component of that in Vancouver."

"As far back as the 1950s, would you say?"

"Oh, sure." There was no hesitation in her answer. "And much, much before that. Say, is there any reason you're focusing on that aspect? Anything you want to tell me?"

"Oh, no. It's just...interesting, is all. There's no reason."

That wasn't true, of course. There was a reason. I just wasn't ready to tell her yet.

There was too big a chance that I was wrong. But now I had some pieces, though none of them seemed to make much sense together. It felt like having parts of half a dozen different jigsaw puzzles. Put those pieces together, and you had a confusing mess. That's what I had now.

A respected Vancouver architect, now dead, with a possible Mafia tie-in. His desk, with old and *remarkable* wine hidden inside. A much younger man who actually bore a resemblance to the architect and who was perhaps involved in some sort of shady stock deal.

One thing was in my favor. Rosa had said MacLeish was in remand, so I knew where he was. Since I had no other real leads, it had occurred to me to try to talk with him. I thought an interaction might offer up some information that would help me make sense of the confusing puzzle pieces.

As a layperson, I would not have been able to gain access to MacLeish, who was in lockup at the downtown Vancouver police station. But my press status enabled me to set up an interview. I scheduled it for the following day at 11 AM. The duty officer was reluctant. But my credentials were in order, even if the whole "Nicole at Night" thing established that I was pretty lightweight. It was enough to get me in the door. The rest would be up to me.

That night I had two more-important-than-usual events to attend, and Kyle had told me he'd like to tag along. Even though he's not a journalist, he doesn't have anything against free food and drinks, and I'd told him I'd be glad of the company. The paper didn't mind if I brought someone along to events, as long as I got my pictures and filed my stories.

Since Kyle's Volvo is nicer than my domestic hatchback, he offered to pick me up. I was still getting ready when he got there, and I buzzed him up and left him to his own devices in my not-so-palatial digs.

"MacLeish." It was his tone more than the name that alerted me. I poked my head out of the bathroom and saw him at my laptop. A violation, but not a major one between brother and sister.

"Yes," I said, coming up behind him. He was looking at my notes. I'd included a copy of one of the microfiche photos of Morrison Brine and his sons. And I'd gotten my hands on the booking photo that had been taken of MacLeish the day before. "That's who was trying to buy my desk," I said. "The one who got arrested at the auction house."

"Come on, Nic. You didn't recognize him?"

I looked from Kyle to the photo and back again.

"Recognize him?" I repeated, clueless. But something was beginning to dawn on me.

"It's Joey MacLeish, Nic. When we were growing up, I'm sure he spent more time at our house than he did at his own."

The mug shot didn't do much to enhance the face I'd seen briefly at the auction house, but now that Kyle mentioned it, I did see… something. When I searched my memory, matching the name with a face from my childhood, I came up with a scraggly beanpole of a kid. He had often lounged around the house with my brother. But they were older than me, and bolder, so I hadn't paid too much attention. Sometimes even on purpose. But, yes, when I thought about it, and when I studied the eyes closely, I could see it.

"When did you guys lose touch?"

"Oh, geez," Kyle said, thinking. "We were still in high school. We fell in with different crowds. His was faster—you know how it goes. Mine was more geeky art types."

And the next thing you know, you turn around and you're looking at a mug shot. Life is like that sometimes.

Kyle and I went to the events as planned, of course. I had a job to do. But both of us were a little sad after that.

SEVEN

I woke up early and excited the next morning. My first real in-person interview for a story. The ones I did for my column were different. A few casual words with glasses of wine between me and my subject, music blaring. Notes dashed off to myself on my phone (usually emailed to myself so I knew where to find them). And, very occasionally, I might follow up one of those impromptu questions with an email or a phone call to confirm a quote. This was different. This, I told myself, might matter.

I dressed carefully. Then rethought the outfit and wore something entirely different. All the while knowing that what I wore would have no bearing on anything at all.

Still.

I got to the downtown lockup half an hour early. It was an immense maze of a building, and I wasn't confident I'd be able to find my way around. I stood in front of the enormous putty-colored building for a few minutes, calming myself before I went in. This is it, I said to myself. A turning point. I was a real reporter now—or I would be soon. I was reporting. Doing what I had been trained to do.

I kept my voice even when I stood in front of the long oak counter and announced myself to the guard.

"I'm Nicole Charles from the *Vancouver Post*," I said with all the authority I could muster. "I have an appointment. I'm here to interview Joseph MacLeish."

The guard looked at me, blinking one, two, three times. He reminded me of a turtle. When he checked the computer, the way he stretched his neck and carefully turned his head made him seem even more turtle-like. I was afraid he was going to mention the whole "Nicole at Night" thing, like so many people did. But if he recognized me, he didn't say anything.

"There's no Joseph MacLeish here," he said after a ridiculously long time.

"But I made an appointment," I said lamely.

One, two, three more blinks. "Even so," he said, "there's no MacLeish here. I checked the record. More than once."

Within minutes I was back on the pavement, exactly where I'd been less than half an hour before with my hopes high and my plans polished. And now I just had another dead end.

A few phone calls verified my suspicions. The charges had been dropped. If Rosa Itani was right and Mafia-types *were* involved, it seemed possible someone had enlisted a smart lawyer to get MacLeish sprung. My timing had been bad.

When I called Kyle to tell him that I had been too late to talk with MacLeish, he was surprisingly sanguine.

"Maybe I know how we can find him," he said, sounding a little smug.

"You do? How? You have some of the same buddies?"

"No. As I told you, we do not. And haven't for quite some time. No. What I'm suggesting is we find him through his mom."

"His *mom*," I said. "I didn't even think about him having one."

"Everyone has one, Nic."

"You know what I mean."

He did. And so we tracked her down. Kyle remembered her well. Though Joey MacLeish had spent a lot of time at our house when he was a kid, Kyle had also spent time at theirs. He remembered Mrs. MacLeish as "delicate and dear," surprising me. Those were soft words from my big brother.

"I think it's possible that their dad wasn't around much. I don't remember him anyway," Kyle said. "But it seems to me his presence was always felt there even so." I understood from the tone that this wasn't necessarily a good thing.

It didn't take us long to find a listing for an S. MacLeish on Capitol Drive in Burnaby. "That would be it, right? That's pretty close to our house."

"Yes," my brother said, nodding with some satisfaction, "that's the address I remember."

"Should we call or go by?"

"Let's go by," he said without hesitation. "Phone would be too weird."

It took a long time for Sari MacLeish to open the door after we rang. She was a dishwater blond, though I guessed her natural hair color now would be gray. I wasn't sure if what she was wearing was part of a peignoir set or some type of weird sweater, but I decided not to think too much about it.

"Mrs. MacLeish?" Kyle said through the screen door.

She peered at Kyle, trying to place him. And then she peered at me, hoping that might add information. It did not.

There was a thin beauty about her, like we were seeing it from the wrong end of a lens. But her sea-green eyes were clear, and when she looked at us there was nothing fuzzy about her at all.

She extended one long finger in Kyle's direction. "I know you," she said. It wasn't a question.

"Kyle Charles," my brother said. "And this is my sister, Nicole. We were Joe's friends. In school."

She seemed to brighten visibly at this.

"Oh yes. I *do* remember you, Kyle. Your smile! Would you like to come in?"

It was a nice house, and it had a lovely view. The living room she led us to was large and luxurious, but even I, who had never been there before, could see that furniture was missing. For one thing, the room was too sparse. For another, there were places where the carpet was darker than it was in other spots. You didn't need to be a detective to see that large pieces of furniture had been removed. It was apparent to me that Joe MacLeish's mom had hit on hard times.

"Do you see Joe very often?" I asked.

"Oh yes," she said. "I see him all the time."

"Have you seen him in the last few days?" I asked. Kyle shot me a glance.

"Why?" she asked, instantly alert. "Is something wrong?"

"No, no," Kyle said. "It's just…we've lost touch, and I've got some information that might be of interest to him."

"It's about a desk," I said, watching her carefully. Nothing. "And Morrison Brine." She lit up when she heard the name. It was like watching a slot machine hit a jackpot.

"That good-for-nothing reprobate!" Kyle and I sat up straighter and exchanged wide-eyed glances. There was no mistaking the tone. "I heard he finally died, didn't he? Good riddance!"

"You weren't friends?" I ventured.

She laughed. It wasn't a happy sound. "I would not say so. No." I was thinking we weren't going to get much more out of her when she surprised us both by speaking again. "He gave me so much, but then he took it all back again. That's the kind of man he was."

"What kind, Mrs. MacLeish?"

But I could see she was thinking about something else. "Wait," she said. "You guys are here about Joe. *And* you're talking about Morrie. What's he done? What's Joe done? Please tell me he's all right."

The rising panic was easy to see. I flashed on the feeling of fear I'd had for my parents. She was concerned for her son. But what did she think he might have done? It hadn't been until we'd started talking about Brine and connected him with Joe that her concern had shown up. Did she know something? I wondered. Was there some reason Joe would go after something of Brine's?

"We have no reason to believe anything has happened to Joe," I told her. "But we do believe he might have gotten himself mixed up with something to do with Brine or his estate."

I saw one spidery hand move to her throat and gently touch her clavicle. A gesture of deep thought. And maybe of worry.

"It's my fault," she said so quietly that I had to lean forward to hear her. "If anything has happened to Joe, it's my fault."

"Why do you think that, Mrs. MacLeish?"

She looked from me to Kyle and back again, as if searching for a way out. I was sure she could not see one.

"I told him." Her voice was even quieter now. Whatever she was holding back was taking its toll.

"What did you tell him?" This was Kyle, matching her quiet tone.

"About Morrie. Morrie and me."

"You were lovers," I said.

She looked at me with alarm. "Certainly not! The very thought…"

There was something in her tone, or maybe in her eyes. I didn't believe her. Not quite.

"But I worked for him after Joe's dad died," she said. "And we became friends."

"When you spoke of him a few minutes ago, it didn't sound like you liked him very much." I said this as gently as possible.

"Oh, that came much later. When I worked for him, we got on well enough. And as I said, over the years we became friends. Okay"—she dipped her head, and I could see a pale pink darken her cheeks—"more than friends. There. I've said it. We were, for a time, in love."

"Morrison was Joe's father," I said.

"Nicole!" This was Kyle.

But Sari MacLeish didn't say anything. She just let her head fall forward, her hair moving with the motion and covering her face from my view. She sat quietly, as if thinking about what to say next. About what might be the right thing to say.

"I guess it doesn't matter now, does it?" In the silence of the room, her voice had startled me slightly. I'd been listening to the echoes of our breathing. "The secrets I've been holding." That shrug again. And a sigh. "Morrie is dead. My son is grown. And it turns out that so many of the things I thought were important were not."

"Do you know how we can get in touch with Joey, Mrs. MacLeish? We'd just like to talk with him."

She hesitated, and Kyle pressed.

"We don't want anything bad for him, Mrs. MacLeish. Remember—we were good friends at school."

I felt her concede before I saw it. A sort of intake of breath that seemed to make her smaller in the end. But she nodded and drew out her phone. "I will call him."

Sari called her son while Kyle and I sat there. We could see her working to convince him. Finally, Joe agreed to meet with us at his mother's house at six, which was a few hours away

Since we were close to our parents' place, Kyle and I ended up going there and hanging out with them rather than going back into the city. Time to catch up on family news and eat a meal and just enjoy our parents a little bit in the meantime. It seemed we did this too infrequently now that we were grown and out of the house and in our own lives. And maybe there had been something about spending time with Joey MacLeish's mom that had made us both crave the company of our own parents. She'd seemed so small somehow. And vulnerable. We didn't discuss it, Kyle and I. Just motored toward our parents' place as soon as we were out of Sari's house.

I was glad to see that things were calmer than they had been on our last visit. Mom and Dad were in the kitchen, preparing a simple meal, when we arrived.

"So wonderful to see you both," my mother enthused when we came in. "And it's an easy matter to make a bit more so you can eat with us, all right?"

My mother is a stellar person in all ways. And she is a terrific mom. But she is not a great cook. That might be due to heritage more than talent or lack thereof. It's true that Scottish food is getting better, but she left Scotland years before that was so. She cooks just about everything long enough to make it soft. It's not always the best approach.

With the sudden appearance of her two chicks home for the evening meal, she replaced the bacon butties she'd been making ("*We can have a sandwich any old day of the week. With my wee ones here,*

I need ta make a meal!") with mince and tatties. Which means she'd been planning on making bacon sandwiches. But with us home she would make hamburger stew with mashed potatoes instead.

Kyle and I winced at the mention of mince and tatties. It was a family standard. Essentially, gray hamburger in its own gray sauce, with a fleck of carrot thrown in for the vegetable component. It is served with boiled and unseasoned potatoes, mashed to a coarse pulp. But today, the four of us enjoyed the meal as much as we used to when Kyle and I were kids. It was like tasting childhood on our tongues.

"So you think it might have been Joseph MacLcish what broke into our house," my mom said at the dinner table when we told her what we were up to. "Well, doesn't that take all? I remember him. Why, I think he even spent a Christmas or two with us. Imagine!"

"Well, not Joe himself," I said. "We know he was in jail when your house was broken into."

"But maybe someone who worked for or with him," said Kyle.

"I oughta give that boy a hiding," my dad huffed.

"I don't think that's necessary, Dad," I told him. "He's been through enough already from the sounds of things."

"Anyway," Kyle chimed in, "we're seeing him afterward. If it comes to pass that it *was* something to do with him, we'll convey your displeasure."

"Right," Dad said. I could see he was only half kidding. "You have my permission to do so."

Our mother was not so easily diverted. "What I don't understand is this," she said. "If it *was* young Joseph, or at his direction, why search everywhere? If it's as you say, you'd have thought he would look for the desk, then leave when he did not find it. But you saw the place. Whoever it was made a right mess."

I'm not sure I stopped with a bite of food in midair, but it felt that way. "Mom's right," I said to Kyle. "As she said, he attended Christmases here. And too many nights and meals to count. He knew his way around our house. Besides, he was like family at that time. Everyone thought so. The Joe I remember would not have ordered someone to break into our home."

"People change," Kyle said darkly. Dad echoed the sentiment with a firm nod.

"Well, we'll see anyway. When we meet with him, just keep an open mind. In any case, everything seems different now. Knowing what we know."

"How do you mean?" Kyle asked.

"Well, Joe's mom. Look how she's living. However this all came about, she has more of a claim to that wine than I do, and it could make a huge difference in her life. It's been bugging me anyway. It's a real conflict of interest in terms of my job. This is my story. And here I am again, right in the middle of it."

"It's your call for sure, Nic. It was always going to be yours. You bought the desk."

"Well, I might be able to make an argument that it's mine," Mom said, "as I paid for the desk in the first place!"

There was laughter after that. Based partly on the general knowledge that, whatever else was true, Mom would always do the right thing.

After dinner we made our way back to the house on Capitol Drive, where there was now a car in the driveway that hadn't been there earlier.

Seeing Joe again was odd. Despite the strained circumstances, you could tell that Kyle and he had been good friends at one point. And now it was like no time had passed, in that their comfort with each other came back quickly.

"It has been an unusual, unfortunate situation," Joe told us. "When I saw who I was bidding against, it made it very awkward. But there was more at stake."

"You recognized me?"

"I did. And I could see you didn't recognize me. And I was glad, because I had to have that desk."

"Why, Joe?" I asked. "Why did you want it so badly?"

"You have to ask?" he said, and I could see he meant it.

"I do."

"She told you," he said. Then, to Sari: "You told them, didn't you?"

Sari just nodded.

"Well then," he said, a little bit triumphantly. "You see, don't you?"

"I don't, Joe. I'm sorry. Please tell me what I'm missing."

"Well, Brine was…he was…my…father."
This last word was said in a whisper. And
then with more force and voice. "I wanted
something that had been his."

"Wait," I said. Whatever else I had been
expecting, it wasn't this. "Are you saying
you wanted the desk just for the sake of
having it?"

"Yes, that's right. I wanted something
of his. Something…significant."

I had to be clear. "You mean you only
wanted it because it was your father's desk?"

Another nod.

"But then why have my parents' place
tossed? If you didn't know about the wine."

I didn't need an answer from him. I
could see from his reaction that he didn't
know what I was talking about, something
he confirmed right away.

"I don't know anything about any wine,
but if a place needed tossing, I wouldn't
have done it to yours."

"That's what I told her," Kyle said. I didn't contradict him.

"Okay, but if not Joe, then who?" I insisted.

"Wait," Sari said. "You're accusing Joe? Is *that* what this is about?"

"It's okay, Mom. I can handle this." He turned to me. "I didn't know anything about any wine. I just wanted my father's desk."

"You were initially charged with false stock promotion. Might someone have thought your bidding on the desk had something to do with that?"

"With the stock? I mean, it's possible, I guess. But I don't really see what or how."

I didn't see it either. It had been a shot in the dark. But I didn't have much else to work with.

EIGHT

I went to the paper and parked myself at one of the unassigned newsroom desks. I hoped that with all the pieces I'd gathered, the larger story would kind of write itself. It did not. There were still more questions than answers.

I opened my file on the case and laid things out on the desk, hoping all of the material I'd accumulated would spark an idea. I'd printed out the photos of MacLeish and Brine and one of my new desk. Then there was the paperwork I'd gotten from the auction house and a clipping of the first story I'd written on the topic. Not a huge cache. As I sat pondering, Mike Webb strolled past my desk. "Who killed the old guy?" he asked, jabbing one thumb toward the photo of Morrison Brine.

"No one," I replied dispiritedly. "He was just old. Nearly ninety."

"That's quite the coincidence, huh?" Mike's voice was mild.

"What is?" I asked, feeling irritated.

Mike answered calmly, "That the guy who is key to your whole deal here kicked off *of natural causes*. What are the odds?" He looked me full in the eyes, smiled, then carried on his way.

I sat there for a full minute after he was gone, letting his words sink in.

Then I picked up the phone.

* * *

It seemed to me that while Morrison Brine had officially died of natural causes, there was a whiff around the whole thing that seemed to leave room for question. His eldest son confirmed that yes, Brine had died at home. Quietly in the night. No, it had not been expected.

"But my father was old," Jefferson Brine said calmly. "And he'd had a full life. We were glad that he went without pain."

"So no autopsy then?"

"No," Jefferson said. "There was no reason. As I said, it was not specifically expected. But at that age…"

"Did you have any reason to suspect foul play?"

"No. Of course not. If we did, we certainly would have done things differently."

"He didn't have any enemies, then? No one who would wish him ill?"

"Not as far as I know."

I hesitated over my last question, and I knew it *would* be my last. But I was the one who wanted to be a reporter. I knew that meant I had to ask hard questions. And so I did. "Mr. Brine, can you confirm for me that your father had dealings with the Mafia early in his career?"

"I think this conversation is over," the younger Brine said.

"Does the name Enzo Rossi mean anything to you?" It was another shot in the dark.

And the line went dead. Which didn't actually confirm anything. But it didn't rule anything out either.

I tried to call Rosa Itani, but she was away from her desk. I left a voice mail and headed out to my car. I didn't have a story. Not yet. But I felt like one was maybe getting close.

* * *

One of the things still bothering me was the tossing of my parents' house. I was certain the search had happened because someone thought the desk was there.

The question was, who would have known that the desk was, technically speaking, owned by my mother? There was only one possible answer. Someone at Lively Auctions.

I'd checked the auction house's website and discovered it was holding a sale that evening. I hoped that meant the place would be fully staffed.

When I got there, the tone was different than on the day I'd bought my desk. A restaurant-supply sale was in progress, and the place was rocking. Not being in the market for a commercial refrigerator or a giant chafing dish, I went straight to the office.

Away from the sale itself, there was only one person working. A young woman whose name tag said she was Jennifer. I recognized her from when I'd paid for the desk. But I could tell she didn't recognize me—mostly because when she lifted her head in my direction, she didn't look straight at me.

Jennifer was wearing pants and a top that both looked two sizes too small. The parts of her that didn't fit oozed beyond the clothing in a way that seemed to threaten the garments' very existence.

"Hey, Jennifer," I started brightly. "My name is Nicole, and I'm a reporter with the *Vancouver Post*. I'm doing an article on buying at auction."

"Really?" She didn't sound impressed.

"Yes, that's right. Can you tell me how the process works?"

"The process?"

"You know. Someone wants to sell something. It goes in the auction. Someone buys something…and so on."

She looked at me like I was from Mars. I had the feeling that as far as she was concerned, I was speaking Martian as well.

"Maybe you wanna talk to Will," she said. Her tone was not helpful.

"Will?"

"He's the auctioneer. But he's busy right now."

Since it was during the auction, I'd come to that conclusion on my own.

Just then the intercom buzzed. "Jennifer, can you bring out the paperwork on that Garland range that came in late? I've got a guy here won't bid without seeing the stove's history."

She rolled her eyes and got busy looking for the paperwork in question. "That's Will. I gotta run this stuff down to him. I'll be back in a minute," she said over her shoulder as she headed for the door. "But I don't think there's anything I can do for you."

As soon as the door whooshed shut behind her, I scooted around to the business side of the desk and sat at the computer. My heart was pounding as my touch brought the machine to life. How long did I have? I really didn't know.

The upside was, what the hell could she do to me besides holler? I tried not to think about it. I didn't want to be hollered at.

It only took a moment to locate the open buyers' files and from there figure out where buyer and seller information was entered. Another two minutes and I'd located the details about the desk I'd bought. I sent the information to the printer, closed the page, and grabbed the printout. Then I scooted around to the correct side of the desk just as Jennifer came back through the door.

I thought she looked at me a little suspiciously, but that might have been my imagination. However, I did *not* imagine her look of pure annoyance when she realized I was still there.

"Really. There's nothing I can do for you tonight. I said that already. Please call Will in the morning." She didn't *tell* me to get out, but I heard it.

"Does he have a direct line? Or maybe you can give me his email address."

Jennifer was irritated enough that she looked at me fully for the first time. When she did, I saw recognition in her eyes. "Say," she said, "weren't you here a few days ago? Buying something?"

I wasn't pleased to be caught out. I'd been pretty sure she wouldn't remember me. "Yes. I was."

"Well, what is this? Some sort of shake-down? Are you a reporter or a customer?"

"Um...both, I guess. Listen, thanks for your time." I was backing toward the door. You've been very helpful."

NINE

There were two reasons for my little attempt at intrigue. One, I wanted to see if it was possible for a random stranger to find out who had consigned or purchased an item at Lively Auctions. And that, at least, I'd proven could be done. Not through the front door maybe. But if I'd managed it, I was sure somcone else could too.

Two, and most important, I'd wanted to see who had consigned the desk in the first place. After all, I knew it hadn't been Morrison Brine himself, since he was dead.

Now, with the hard-won document in my hand, I had what I needed. I walked to my car, fearful that someone would stop me. No one did.

I drove three blocks, then pulled onto a side road to look it over. It was not surprising to me that Jefferson Brine was the consignor, but it *was* a little sad. An acknowledged son barely waiting for his father to be cold in the ground before getting rid of his most beloved possessions. The unacknowledged son in the end putting himself at risk to buy one thing that his father had cared about.

Knowing who had consigned the desk was interesting but not helpful. But knowing who had wanted what was *in* the desk—that was a different matter.

I was sitting there in my car when the phone rang. It was Rosa, returning my call.

"Don't get me wrong, kid," she said. "I love talking to you. But I do have to make time for other people too, you know."

I laughed. "Okay. Point taken. But I think I'm getting somewhere."

"With what?"

"Morrison Brine. Joseph MacLeish. Et cetera."

"Ah. Right. Okay. What have you got?"

"I think someone killed Morrison Brine."

I heard her typing in the background

"Nic, says here Brine was nearly ninety. I mean, a stiff breeze can kill you at that age."

"Still. It fits. He'd been making enemies for a lotta years. And whoever killed him wanted what was in the desk I bought. But his son sold the desk before they could get what they needed out of it. So then they found out my mom paid for the desk and went to her house and tossed it."

"You got your mom to buy your desk?"

"That wasn't really the point of the story, Rosa. I had trouble with a card, and... well, never mind that. It doesn't matter.

What *does* matter is someone went to her house and tossed it. They were looking for something."

"Okay, just stop for a second. Where does Joseph MacLeish fit into your whole scheme here?"

"MacLeish was Brine's illegitimate son."

"Of course he was," Rosa said jovially. "Why the hell not?"

"That part I can prove. Anyway, Joe just wanted the desk because it had been his dad's. But he didn't know there was priceless wine in the desk…"

"What?"

"And someone else—I don't know who—knew about the wine and the desk and wanted to get their hands on it."

"And you have evidence to support all of this?"

"Well…not exactly."

"Not exactly?"

"Okay, barely at all."

"Listen, Nic, you're a good kid. And I know you don't mean to be wasting my time with this stuff, but this city is pretty busy with actual crimes getting committed. As much as I like chatting with you—and I *do*—hon, this one is unsupportable. You've got public figures getting killed by God knows who. And from what you've told me you've got pretty close to zero evidence of anything other than you bought a desk."

"And my parents' place was broken into."

"Okay. And that. But the rest of it? Pretty close to pure conjecture. And I get it—you're a writer. You can make stuff up. Not saying that you mean to, necessarily. But all of this plus five bucks will get you a coffee. I've listened to what you had to say really carefully, and there's just nothing I can act on."

Though my first instinct was to argue, I knew that Rosa had a point. A lot of this stuff was just me doing my little investigations and piecing things together as best as I could. My wanting things to fit together didn't mean they actually would. Maybe there were no answers. Maybe I'd only been pushing so hard because I wanted a story. Maybe there *wasn't* a single story here, just the constant mosaic of stories. I suddenly felt very tired.

When I got off the phone, I pulled my car back onto the road and headed to my favorite sushi joint, where I ate alone at the bar. Over a tekka maki, a California roll and a bowl of miso soup, I contemplated possibilities. But I realized right about then that I was done thinking for the moment. I couldn't see anymore. Maybe things would look brighter in the morning, but for right now, I just wanted to go home.

At my building, I parked the car and trudged up the stairs, my head full of all the unsubstantiated facts I'd found. Suddenly all I wanted was a bubble bath, or maybe a half hour of mindless TV.

I was so intent on my thoughts, I almost didn't notice that the door to my apartment was unlocked.

I pushed the door open, not really thinking things through. "Kyle? Is that you?" I called out. Not even remembering in that moment that my brother does not have a key.

What happened next unfolded so quickly that I can't properly credit it.

A hand came out of nowhere and pushed me down. Firmly enough that I feared I was in danger. I landed with my face on the floor, and I had the presence of mind to not lift my head. Part of me wanted desperately to see who was in my apartment. Part of me knew that my life might well depend on me not doing so.

I heard no voices, was aware only of the sounds of multiple feet. More than one person. The clinking of glass. The wine bottles, of course. And then the desk drawers and the rustling of paper. And as I heard the footfalls recede, down the hall and then down the stairs, I tried to drum up emotion for what was happening. Should I not feel sorrow or regret or sadness? Maybe I did, but in those few minutes that I was free of the burdens the desk had produced, I also felt quickly and strangely released.

The feeling didn't last long. Before the sounds of the thieves had fully receded, I heard the crash banging of less careful feet. I picked myself up. Ran to the window. Saw half a dozen police cars and a police van fanned out in front of my building. Then heard more sounds on the ground floor beneath me. I could tell the cops were down there, doing their job.

TEN

"You told me you didn't believe me," I said to Sergeant Itani. She was Rosa when we were in her office or on the phone. But here, in uniform and with a whole unit of police officers under her command, and a couple of bad guys in the van, she had to be addressed with respect, even if just in my mind.

"You're right, I didn't," she said. "But after we got off the phone, I did a little digging. Enough of what you said checked out, so I asked a car to swing by, and they found suspicious activity."

"What checked out?"

We were standing out in front of my building. The night air was refreshing after the smell of wood and wax I'd inhaled with my face pressed against the floor.

"Well, for one, it seems possible to me that Morrison Brine's death was not entirely accidental."

"Really?" Of all the things I'd expected to hear, that wasn't one.

"Yeah. And you're right, your parents' place getting broken into was odd. Considering the timing."

"Right?"

"But what really got me thinking was the Mafia connection you suggested. And you were right there too. There were connections hinted at between Brine's success and that of a certain branch of the Rossi family. I looked fast, and the connections I was able to make at a glance wouldn't stand up in court. But it was enough to get me a little worried about all the poking around you've been doing. You never know what kind of hornet's nest you'll stir up with that kind of stuff."

"And here we are."

"Right. And here we are. Now, I'm not sure yet who *those* guys are, but I'm sure they didn't have a key to your place. Am I right?"

"Geez, Rosa, they were in there when I got home. Your timing could not have been better, or they'd have gotten away with the wine."

Rosa looked at me speculatively, as if weighing whether I was pulling her leg. She must have realized I wasn't kidding around, because she shook her head and said, "No wine, hon. Just this."

She led me to a pile of crumpled paper. At first I didn't realize what it was. And then…I sort of did, though not exactly.

"I can tell by your face," she said. "You recognize these."

"Kinda. Not really. They sort of look like the papers the bottles were wrapped in."

Her eyes kind of widened at that, but she didn't say anything at first. Then: "Look more closely."

I did. The papers the bottles had been wrapped in were folded over onto each other. Unfolded, it became clear that each bottle had been wrapped in a sheaf of papers.

"Stock certificates?" I ventured.

Rosa nodded. "Good guess. Go to the head of the class. You recognize the stock?"

"No. Is it the same one Joe was pumping?"

"No. That was some cheap penny stock. That wouldn't have been worth hiding. Or stealing. No. Look more closely."

I did. And then said, almost right away, "These are shares in Enzo Rossi's development company."

"You've got it. We'll have to look at it all more closely, of course, but I'm guessing this is some kind of holding stock we're looking at. Like, not a significant share of the company."

"But valuable?"

"I'd guess so. Based on the fact that these guys didn't knock."

* * *

Finally settled at my desk, a cup of tea cooling at my elbow, my story came together quickly. Oh, there were holes still to be filled in—lots of them—but I was well on my way, the pieces all fitting the way they should. This was the story that would make my career. I just knew it. It had everything—murder, intrigue, high stakes, significant sacrifice. I almost wept while I wrote parts of it. I was so astonished with the deftness of the piece, the variety of elements and my skill at handling it all. Truly, I thought, I was going to be unstoppable. I had trouble keeping my excitement down.

"But I don't think I understand," Kyle said to me when I told him everything. I'd called him before I started writing. Then I'd buzzed him into my building around the time I wrote *-30-* at the bottom of the piece, signifying "the end." I filed the story while he tromped up the stairs. "You mean the wine was never the target? They wanted these stock certificates all along?"

"Well, we don't have all the details yet, but yeah. Something like that." I told him the conclusions in the story I'd written earlier and filed. It would be in the morning edition, a fait accompli.

"So let me get this straight. Someone killed Brine in order to get those stock certificates."

"Looks that way."

"And all that business with Joey and the stocks he was pumping?"

"Coincidence, in a way. Except the fact that Joey was bidding on the desk must have been what made these galoots think the desk held what they wanted."

"I don't understand."

"It was known that Joey was a promoter. There were times he would have inside information on certain stocks—or at least he allowed people to think he did. And it was known that Brine, for whatever reason, had a golden touch. And all of a sudden Joey is bidding on a dead man's desk? It wouldn't have taken much math for them to figure something was going on."

"And they were there, too?"

"Folowing him, yes. That's what I imagine."

"Okay, so that's Joey. How'd they know to come to you?"

"That's been bothering me too. I think it must have been the girl at the auction house. But I guess with all the poking around I was doing, I didn't exactly make my interest a secret."

Once Kyle was gone, and with my story written, I had a strong desire to close this chapter. The chapter of the desk. I wanted a fresh start, everything new. And the feeling of violation, of having been broken into—I wanted that gone as well.

I'd brought home some oil soap from my mom's. She blends it with water and puts it in a special bottle so that you can spray it on wood to clean it. Honestly, if you want something cleaned, ask a Scot. That's been my experience. My mom has a cleaning solution for everything, and bleach figures in a lot of those recipes. For wood, it's oil soap, water and a damp rag. And so I went to work on the desk.

I hummed while I did it, enjoying the rise of the honey-gold color of the wood as I rubbed the oil soap in. After a while the wood seemed to glow. When the outside of the desk was polished and gleaming, I turned to the inside. I pulled out the drawers and cleaned everything I could see or reach, going deep into the corners and lovingly around the dovetail joints.

When I went to push the top drawer back in, it stuck. I tried it this way and that, but I could not put it back where it had been. Something was in the way. I reached in and felt…something. What? The tips of my fingers identified the texture of thick paper—which, it seemed to me, shouldn't be jammed at the back of a desk drawer.

I got out my flashlight. Peered deep inside. And against the pure symmetry of this well-designed piece of furniture, I saw something that didn't quite fit. I reached in as far as I could, but I couldn't quite grab it. I went to the kitchen. Got my longest set of tongs. Reached inside with them and grabbed. I felt a surge of adrenaline as I got hold of whatever it was with the tongs and pulled it out. It felt like victory even before I knew what it was.

The envelope was creamy and thick, with a rich texture. An envelope from another time. *Sari* was written on the front of the envelope in a firm blue hand.

Before I did anything else, I called Kyle.

ELEVEN

Sari MacLeish took the envelope from me with a hand that trembled only slightly. I don't think I would have shown as much composure under the circumstances. Actually, I'm pretty sure I would not.

"And it was in a desk, you say?"

We were at her house again, having called her to let her know what I'd found.

"That's right. A desk I bought at auction last week. It was his. Brine's."

"And it's addressed to me," she said, looking at the envelope, at her name in what

I guessed was his bold printing. There was disbelief in her voice.

"Do you want to read it after we leave? It's all right if you do."

"No. Stay, please. Just for a while."

"Sure," Kyle and I said almost in unison.

I watched her closely as she read. Her face was cloudy as she began, but the more she read, the lighter it seemed to become. It wasn't a long letter, judging by the time it took for her to read it. And by the end, tears ran down her cheeks like spring rain from a clear sky.

"He loved me," she said, wonderment in her voice. "He loved me all along."

"What did he say?" I didn't like to pry, but curiosity was getting the better of me.

"So much. But most of all, he said he should have made different choices. He had regrets." Her voice hardened then, surprising me. Until she spoke. Then I understood.

"Regrets! All those years. What a waste of time."

She was right, of course. Because whatever else it said, the note and his apology indicated a loss there was no coming back from. You can't take it with you, as they say. And when a day is gone, you'll never get it back.

"What a waste of time," she said again. The anger was gone from her voice now. Regret was all I heard. And maybe grief.

* * *

In the morning I got up early and went for a run. I like to run in the morning, but today it was the newspaper I was after. The morning edition. My story in particular, of course. It wasn't front-page stuff. I knew that. But I'd written a good, solid piece that might make a difference in the end.

I got back to my place, made tea in anticipation of reading, then spread the paper out, preparing to find and read my piece. It wasn't anywhere. But an article on page six under my rival Brent Hartigan's byline caught my eye.

Auction-House Event Solves Decades-Old Mystery

Brent Hartigan

And, in very small type, *with files by Nicole Charles.*

I felt a flood of rage, followed by a despair that threatened tears, followed by a near-hysterical urge to laugh. I went with the last of the emotions. If a choice had to be made, it seemed the healthiest of the three.

The article under Brent's byline was my story. And yet it was not. Brent had hit the highlights, and the stuff about the wine had been left out altogether.

I called my editor.

"What the hell, Mike!" I said. I didn't think he'd need me to fill him in. I was right.

"Sorry, Nicole. I know you wanted this story. And your piece…well, honestly, it was okay but not as objective as I needed it to be. You understand."

"It was plenty objective," I said. "And if you needed it to be different, I could have fixed it. Easily."

"Sure, I get it, Nicole. But there just wasn't time…" He said more, but I tuned it out. Everything I needed to know, I'd heard. The rest was just whitewashing—I understood that. He'd known I'd be pissed, and he was right. I wanted to rail at him, but I knew I wouldn't do that. No sense burning bridges or closing doors. In future, there would be a chance for me to get what I wanted. In the meantime, nothing I could say or do would alter what had happened.

So I'd lost another story. Brent Hartigan had gotten another byline. An opportunity for Joe MacLeish had gone astray. But of all of us, I thought Sari MacLeish had suffered the greatest loss. She'd discovered that she'd been loved in return. A useless love for both her and Brine. Years of hurt and loss when there could have been joy.

If the cops ever got around to giving me back the wine, I was thinking I'd give it to Sari. In so many ways, I didn't feel I had a claim to it. And it seemed to me that, as the mother of Brine's child, she really did. I didn't think a few bottles of wine would make everything better. But maybe it would take the edge off. And at this late date? Maybe that was enough.

There was a message in all of this. I tried to decipher it. A lesson to be learned. I thought about it as I drove to the office. Something about taking opportunities when they presented themselves. About watching sunsets when they occurred and taking love and chances when they landed, before it was too late.

I thought again about what Clark had told me when I'd met him at his book launch. About how writing a book made you the expert on a thing. And though I knew I didn't have the experience to do it, I had a sudden urge to be writing about opportunities taken and lost. About how windows open when doors shut, and that satisfaction is for those who drive toward it.

I parked the car and got on the elevator to zoom up to the newsroom. There was a calm determination in my heart. There would be other stories.

AUTHOR'S NOTE

I continue to be proud of my association with Orca Books and the good work it undertakes with its Rapid Reads program. The challenge is significant and worthwhile and if *When Blood Lies* works in all of the ways it is meant to, it is entirely due to the challenges issued and efforts given by the whole team at Orca, in particular my splendid editor Ruth Linka.

A special thanks to the men in my life, Michael Karl Richards, Peter Huber and Tony Parkinson. Your significant and varied contributions add texture, context and substance far beyond what you know and see.

LINDA L. RICHARDS is a journalist and award-winning author. She is the founding editor of *January Magazine*, one of the Internet's most respected voices about books. She is also the author of six other novels and several works of nonfiction and is on the faculty of the Simon Fraser University Summer Publishing Workshops. In 2010, Richards's novel *Death Was in the Picture* won the Panik Award for Best Los Angeles-Based Noir. For more information, visit www.lindalrichards.com or @lindalrichards.

A Nicole
Charles
Mystery

If It
Bleeds

LINDA L. RICHARDS

More than anything, Nicole Charles wants to be a real reporter. She didn't go to journalism school to work the society pages. One night while covering a gallery opening, she discovers a dead body in a dark alley. Suddenly Nicole is right in the middle of the biggest story of the year. It's the chance of a lifetime. Too bad someone had to die to make it happen.

"Like any well written novella, author, Richards hooks the reader within thirty seconds: west coast Vancouver atmosphere, tight plot, judicious back story, dialogue and a body. Add the tension of a newsroom full of testosterone, egos and dubious fair play and you get...*If It Bleeds*...read it. Hope there is more to come."

—Don Graves

RAPID READS
WWW.RAPID-READS.COM